OMG... IS HE ALSO A WITCH?!

Talia Aikens-Nuñez

TO MY LITTLE WITCHES...

Published by Central Avenue Publishing, an imprint of Central Avenue Marketing Ltd.
www.centralavenuepublishing.com

Published in Canada
Printed in United States of America

1. JUVENILE FICTION/Fantasy & Magic 2. JUVENILE FICTION / Girls & Women

Lexile® measure: 520L

CHAPTER 1

BAM! April jolted awake and sat straight up. *What was that noise?* Swinging her legs over the side of the bed, she hopped to her feet. She wiped her eyes and grabbed her glasses from the desk. She shuffled to the window and pressed her face against the glass, her eyes scanned back and forth. *I can't see anything.* The fog was as thick as pancake syrup.

She blinked her eyes. *What is that?* Standing at the end of her driveway was a figure. *Is that an animal? It's too big to be a squirrel. It's not a deer.* Squint. Focus. *Is that a person?* The figure moved. Her breath quickened, fogging up the window. *Ugh*! She used her hand to wipe the window so she could see outside.

The wind whooshed. Leaves on the trees flipped and flapped in the October wind. Close to the ground, the fog thinned out like strands of cotton candy being pulled apart. The bottom of the figure became clearer. Black pants. The fog lifted a bit more. Black shirt. The fog still covered the face. April slowly slid the window up and carefully pressed her face against the screen. The shadowed, ghostly figure took a few steps forward. *OMG...is that a boy*? *Why is he standing there?* He was staring up at the large tree that stood next to her house. "Fall," he commanded.

A loud, cracking sound filled the night air. Her heart raced. *Where'd he go? What's he doing? I can't see anything!* She pushed up the screen to stick her head out of the window. She looked left. She looked right. Then she looked down at her father's SUV, his 'dream car.' Mrs. Appleton would jokingly say, "Your dad loves that car more than he loves me!"

Her eyes widened. *Boom-boom, boom-boom,* pounded her heart. Lit now by the motion light on the garage and the full moon, April could see her father's car was crushed by the large branch that had hung over their driveway. *Oh no! Dad will be so upset. Who was that? What should I do? Should I go tell Mom and Dad?* Before she got to her feet to go get her parents, she remembered, *Wait! I am a witch, I can fix this!*

She looked under her bed and saw her spell book, the *Book of Magie,* resting there. As a young witch who accidentally discovered that she has magical powers, she received the spell book from her trusted French-speaking friend, Eve, who moved here from New Orleans. Eve wasn't a witch but her grandmother was. Her *grand-mère*, which is French for grandmother, owned the ancient French spell book when she was alive and then passed it on to Eve. Now that April had these powers, Eve believed the book was better off with April.

April reached under her bed to touch the cover of the *Book of Magie.* Now that she had done a few successful spells and taken a French class, she was pretty good at reading the spells with some help from her French-English dictionary.

She carefully slid out the heavy, leather-bound book and stared at it. *This book is so cool*, she thought as her finger ran down its brown cover and raised, braided trim. It reminded her of old books she'd seen at garage sales. The pages were as thin as tissue paper and she would read the spells when she was alone in her room.

She turned on the small desk lamp then knelt back down on the floor. Carefully turning the pages, she thought, *I know I saw something in here about repairing broken trees, plants and rocks.* She took a deep breath in; the book released an old-library odor as she turned the pages. *Here it is!*

At the top of a page halfway through the book was a spell with a pencil drawing of a tree split in half. She read the French title, *Réparer. A spell 'to repair', perfect.* She translated more of the spell as she read.

Maintenir l'élément que vous essayez de réparer dans votre main.

Hold the element that you are trying to fix in your hand. Huh, element? The pencil drawing showed a picture of a woman holding a small branch in her hand as she looked at the broken tree. *Oh, I get it, hold something wooden to repair the tree and something metal to repair the car.*

I can't get a branch from outside because the alarm beeps when the door is opened. I have to find something in here. Her eyes searched the dimly lit room. Everything was in its place. Her stuffed animals, clothes, the chandelier. *That's it!* She spotted the three-foot-long walking stick made from a branch at camp last summer. It was squeezed between her stuffed animals and covered in pink glitter and streamers. She grabbed it, and continued to scan the room for something metal. *Ah, yes.* She spotted the metal cup engraved with her name: April Isabella Appleton. Holding the cup in her other hand, her eyes went back to the spell book.

Repeat twice with your eyes closed:

The tree is what I want to repair,
Fixing the damage at which I stare.
Heal the ruin, mend what I see,
Cure all of the harm brought by the tree.

She stood up and looked out the window. The haze still covered the crushed car. She took a deep breath, closed her eyes and repeated the spell twice more:

The tree is what I want to repair,
Fixing the damage at which I stare.
Heal the ruin, mend what I see,
Cure all of the harm brought by the tree.

The tree is what I want to repair,
Fixing the damage at which I stare.
Heal the ruin, mend what I see,
Cure all of the harm brought by the tree.

Tight knots formed in her stomach. Wiping her sweaty palms on her pajama pants, she cracked one eye open. She slowly opened her other eye and the tree was repaired. *Perfect, it's back to normal!* Her father's car sat under the branch, unharmed.

April's shoulders relaxed as she exhaled. *Being a witch is pretty cool. I can stop people from hurting our things. Hmm, I wonder who that boy was?* She put the *Book of Magie* back under her bed, making sure it was safe and secure. Climbing back into bed, she took a deep breath, but could not calm down. April flipped around to her other side. *Who was that boy? Why would he do that?* Her heart still beating hard, she took another deep breath.

She closed her eyes but could not get the image of the boy out of her head. After an hour of flip-flopping and taking more deep breaths, she finally fell asleep.

CHAPTER 2

"OH NO!" Mr. Appleton yelled.

April's eyes popped open. *Dad never yells. What's going on?*

"Abbey! Abbey! Can you come down here?" Her father yelled up the stairs to April's mother.

Mrs. Appleton came to the top of the stairs.

"Honey, what's wrong?" April's mother asked.

April's stomach fell. Jumping to her feet, she ran to the window. She covered her eyes. *Please say it was a dream. Please say it was a dream.*

She squeezed her eyes shut and held her breath for several moments. Hearing nothing, she slowly relaxed her face, dropped her arms and then opened her eyes. *I fixed it. I know I did.*

April stood at the window, squinting as the golden morning light poured through. Even though she was a witch, she was still pretty new at it. She thought about all the chaos that becoming a witch had caused in the past. She remembered her first spell of mistakenly turning her pestering brother, Austin, into a dog. Next, she remembered all the elephants that appeared in her town, causing destruction and mayhem, when all she wanted was to help them. Without the help of Eve and Grace, she would never have been able to undo either of those spells. Just when she thought she had better control of her powers, this happened. *Did my spell not work? No. I saw the tree mended. Did someone undo my spell? Did someone steal the* Book of Magie? All these questions made her head spin.

She reached for her glasses on the desk and put them on. The lump in her throat grew. She looked under the bed, the book was still there. *Phew, it's safe!* Daring a look out the window, she saw it. Her father's dream car was crushed by a massive branch, the one she thought she repaired. She remembered that boy in black. *How could he do this?*

"OMG… Is he also a witch?!"

CHAPTER 3

MR. APPLETON paced back and forth across the driveway. His cell phone was glued to his ear. From her window, April saw his arm waving, his face grew redder and redder with each minute that passed. *Boy, he's angry. I wish I could fix it again now. But, then I'd have to explain to them how I did that.* Her stomach churned at that thought. *Never mind.*

Well, he definitely can't give me a ride to school today. I better hurry to get the bus. She threw on her clothes. Racing down the stairs, she grabbed her backpack. "Bye, Mom."

Mrs. Appleton stood at the kitchen sink as still as a statue. April realized her mom didn't hear her. Mrs. Appleton held her cup of coffee and stared out the window at Mr. Appleton's car. April stopped and looked out the same window. The roof of the car was completely caved in. The branch was longer than the length of the car. It lay across the flattened roof and deeply dented the hood. The bumper dangled off the front.

April's pulse quickened. *Who was that boy? Why was he trying to cause such trouble? Gosh, I hope I didn't cause this.* She hated seeing her dad so upset and her mom so worried.

"Bye, Mom," April said louder.

"Oh, sorry, honey." Her mom came over to her, still wearing her bathrobe and slippers.

"You have to take the bus today. Okay?"

Mrs. Appleton asked.

April nodded.

"Have a good day at school, sweetie." Mrs. Appleton kissed April on her forehead then glanced at the clock. It read 7:15am. "Oh, you better hurry. You have five minutes until the bus gets to the corner."

"I know. I'll meet Grace there. Um, Mom?"

"Yes?" Her mom raised one eyebrow.

"Is Dad okay?"

April's mom stroked April's cheek and smiled at her. "Well, Dad is safe. That's the most important thing. He's just angry right now. But, he'll be fine."

"Dad love-love-loved that car!"

"Yep, he always called it his 'dream car', didn't he?" Mrs. Appleton's smile faded. "But, we will get another. Insurance will pay for it." A small grin appeared on her face.

Her mother's peaceful presence had a

calming effect on April. She took a deep breath, looked down at the ground and said, "Okay."

Mrs. Appleton put her finger under April's chin and lifted her daughter's head to look her in the eye. "I can see that you're worried. He'll be fine. You know what I always say?"

"There's no space in your heart for fear." Both April and her mom said this at the same time. Mrs. Appleton always had sayings she would teach April and Austin. April had no idea how her mom remembered all of those sayings. She would say things like: 'Home is where the heart is,' and, 'A wise person makes her own decisions and doesn't follow others,' and 'Logic will get you from A to Z, but imagination will get you everywhere.'

Mrs. Appleton's broad smile made April grin. She kissed April on the forehead. "Time to get to school. Go on to the bus stop, I want to mop this floor before I go to work."

April took a step toward the door.

“Wait, don’t forget your house key.” Her mom picked the key off the hook next to the kitchen door that opened to the driveway. She slid it into April’s pocket and smiled at her. “Don’t lose it.”

April smiled at her mom and walked out the door. As she ran down the driveway, she could hear her father’s agitated voice as he talked on the phone. “For crying out loud, can you please get a tow truck and a replacement car here? Please! I need to get to work.”

April swallowed hard. She peered over her shoulder to look at her father.

“Bye, Dad.”

He stopped pacing and looked up. Seeing April, he forced a smile. “Bye, honey. No ride today.” He pointed to the crushed car. “But, I love you.”

April smiled at him and pointed at the

corner. “It’s okay. I’ll take the bus. I love you too.”

Then her father said sternly into the cell phone, “Yes, I’m still here.”

He continued walking back and forth.

CHAPTER 4

WHEN April reached the bus stop, Grace was already there. Grace was halfway through her word find book. Word games and brain teasers were her favorites.

Grace stared at her book, feverishly circling words. "I saw your Dad having a bit of trouble this morning."

Since Grace lived next door to April, she always knew what was going on in her house. Not only had she been April's best friend for a long time, she also helped get April out of trouble when her spells went awry.

Grace, ever the detective, continued her interrogation. "I find it weird because there was some fog last night but no wind or storm." Grace looked up at April and started tapping the pen against the book. "Is there something you would like to tell me?"

"You really have to go into the FBI or CIA when you grow up. You'd be the best investigator," April quipped.

Grace gave a wide, Cheshire Cat grin. "Now, spill. What did you do?"

April's heart raced again. "I didn't do anything. I promise."

Grace glared at April. "Really?"

April cleared her throat. "But, I did see something."

The bus pulled up in front of the girls. They found seats next to Eve. As they sat down,

Eve gave them a huge smile, her tan skin was almost glowing. Eve was so charming with her Cajun accent and outgoing personality. "The sun is shining and the birds are chirping. It's a beautiful day. Right, girls?" She nearly sang the greeting.

Grace scowled at her. It was funny to watch since Grace was not a morning person and it irritated her that Eve was always so cheerful this early in the day.

"Sure, whatever," Grace said with a pained look. "I have math first thing with mean old Mr. Malus."

The smile faded from Eve's face. "Yeah, I have him after lunch. We have a test on fractions."

"Ugh, I really don't like that guy. He's only been here a month and I already can't stand him." Grace groaned.

April agreed. "He always seems super creepy

when he is hunched over his bowl of whatever he eats in the cafeteria at lunch."

All three girls giggled.

"Hey, before we get to school I have to tell you what happened last night." April motioned for the girls to huddle close. Both Eve and Grace knew all about April's abilities. While they weren't witches, they helped her before, and she knew she could trust them with all of her secrets.

"I woke up in the middle of the night. There was rustling and a bang. I looked out the window. There was a boy standing at the end of the driveway. I think *he* made that huge branch fall on my dad's car."

Eve gasped, "*Mon Dieu!*"

Grace leaned in closer to April and whispered. "So, was it a ghost or are you saying there is another witch in our town besides you?"

April gravely nodded her head.

CHAPTER 5

THE bus let the girls off in front of the school. They walked up the steps to the front door. Typically, Mrs. Ramirez, the principal, greeted everyone as they came into school. Her cheerful face could always be found at the door for arrival and for dismissal. She was a sweet lady and wore clothes that reflected the season, like scarves with Valentine hearts on them, Easter Bunny leggings and ugly Christmas sweaters.

Things seemed different this morning. Mrs. Ramirez's usually neatly braided hair was pulled into a sloppy bun. She looked sweaty despite the cool morning air and she was missing her Halloween-themed clothing.

"What's wrong?" April asked as Mrs. Ramirez nervously picked at her nails.

"Oh, nothing for you kids to worry about. Just a little problem with the heat." Mrs. Ramirez looked down at the girls.

As they walked through the door, there was a blast of extremely hot air. Instantly, beads of sweat formed on their foreheads.

"I believe the classrooms are cooler. Just the hall and bathrooms are a *bit* warmer," Mrs. Ramirez said.

"A 'bit' warmer?" Eve gasped.

"Why is it so hot?" Grace said, ballooning her shirt to cool herself off.

"Well...," Mrs. Ramirez started. She

crinkled up her nose and seemed to be lost in thought. "Don't worry, this heat thing should be fixed shortly."

Mrs. Ramirez looked over the girls' heads out the large windows around the front doors of the school. "I am waiting for the repair people to arrive, any minute now." Her eyes grew large. "I think I see them. Okay, girls, get to class." Mrs. Ramirez darted out the doors waving at the team of workers walking toward the school.

The girls walked down the hall to their classrooms. Eve looked at April with her lashes fluttering. "My eyes are so dry I think my eyelids will get stuck."

"OMG, sweat is going to start pouring off of me like Niagara Falls," Grace said, disgusted.

April fanned herself with her notebook. "I haven't sweat this much since Field Day last year."

In spite of the heat, a chill suddenly went down April's back. *Is someone watching me*? She looked around. Lots of kids were fanning themselves as they walked to class.

Out of the corner of her eye, she saw someone standing in the entrance to the gym. She whipped her head around. There stood the new boy in her class, David. He had dark skin and carried a suede book bag embroidered with beads. His straight, black hair was pulled into a low ponytail. He looked at her inquisitively. She turned away and kept walking down the hall. A pit formed in her stomach. Ever since discovering she was a witch, she could tell when something bad was about to happen.

Right now, she had that feeling.

CHAPTER 6

"OKAY, I have to get some water." Grace stopped at the water fountain. "My mouth is as dry as it is when I eat the cafeteria's bread." Grace bent down to sip some water. She splashed some on her face. "Ah, that feels better."

"Taking a shower in the water fountain?" April smirked.

"Ha ha," Grace sneered, turning toward their classroom as water dripped from her face and hands.

Boom! Grace fell to the floor on her bottom. "Ouch!"

"Oh dear, you must have slipped on all that water you just splashed everywhere," Eve said, walking over to Grace.

"Or, I slipped on the sweat dripping from everyone else," Grace said with her usual sense of humor as she looked at the other kids.

"Let me help you up," David said. He had appeared in front of Grace with his arm extended.

A bit shocked, Grace looked up and her face went red. She smiled and stretched out her hand. He helped her up.

"Thank you. Well, this is embarrassing," she said with a chuckle.

"Don't worry about it. Are you okay?" David's large, dark brown eyes focused on Grace with concern.

"I think so." She looked down at the ground, biting her lower lip. "But, it's as hot as the Sahara in here, geesh."

"Totally!" David laughed good-naturedly along with Grace.

"Umm, okay. Well, I better get to class. But, I'll dry my face off first." Grace chuckled and wiped her face on her shirt sleeve.

"Good idea." He winked, turned around and walked down the hall.

"Let's get to the classrooms, Mrs. Ramirez said it's cooler in there." April urged them down the hall after David.

"Ugh, there is that totally evil math teacher. One time he told me he couldn't read my writing so he marked all of my math problems as wrong. I mean, really! I offered to go to the computer and type it out for him. But, he said no." Eve nodded her head at where Mr. Malus was standing.

"Wow! That is evil. I heard that last week he

gave a girl a zero on her homework because she used pen instead of pencil. I guess he doesn't like pen." Grace rolled her eyes.

"Geesh, that is mean. You know, I heard his first name is Norn. That is one weird name. I am so happy I don't have him," April said.

Grace and Eve stopped walking. They turned around to glare at April. "We do!"

"Sorry." April grinned.

Mr. Malus stood at the entrance to his classroom; his tall, skinny body dressed all in black and an odd necklace around the collar of his shirt. He stared at David who walked down the hall to another classroom. The girls were a few steps behind him. As David approached Mr. Malus, the teacher rubbed the charm on his necklace and said something quietly. April watched his lips move. Then he clapped his hands twice.

April looked at her friends but they didn't seem to notice Mr. Malus clap. Then, she saw he and David look at each other and nod. David threw his hands up and exclaimed, "Birds!"

April's knees went weak. *Something is wrong. This feels familiar. Really familiar.* All the blood rushed out of her face. She stopped walking. Everyone else kept walking and talking. Grace and Eve shuffled ahead of her. Tight knots formed in her stomach. *Is he the boy from last night? I know that voice.* "It's him!"

Grace and Eve stopped walking. They turned to look at April. "Oh my, April. You are as white as a ghost. Are you okay, my dear?" Eve asked.

Grace waved her hands in front of April's face. "You're not blinking. Not only are you as white as a ghost, but you look like you just saw one."

The hair rose on the back of April's neck. "It's him," she whispered.

Grace tilted her head to the side. "What? April, you will have to stop the weird talk. Who is *him*?"

"I heard him command 'Birds' like he commanded 'Fall' to make the branch fall on my dad's car. OMG...David is the other witch."

CHAPTER 7

GRACE'S eyes bulged out. "That's crazy. He can't be. He was just so nice to me."

April's glasses slipped down the bridge of her nose and she pushed them back up. "He was, until Mr. Malus clapped his hands."

Eve wrinkled her nose. "Why would he say, 'Birds?'"

AAAAHHHH!

Some kids near the front door started screaming. April, Grace, and Eve turned to look. Kids were running through the front doors into the building.

Mrs. Ramirez followed after them, screaming, "Close the doors! Close the doors!"

She was too late. As she came through the door, a flock of large, black crows swooped into the school. One bird swooped so low it almost hit her in the head. She ducked. *Plop!* One of the birds pooped on a kid next to her.

The large crows flapped their long, black wings. *Caw-Caw, CAW-CAW.* The sound got louder as they flew down the hallway. Swooping and swooshing, bird after bird flew into the school.

With their book bags jostling against their hips, the girls bounded down the hallway toward their classrooms. Things were flying out of kids' bags—lunches, juice boxes, notebooks, pencils. It was chaos.

Bang! April slid on someone's pencil case on

the floor and fell. "Ouch!"

Eve ran back and extended her hand to April. "I never leave a girl behind."

April tried to smile.

"Come on. Up, up," Eve commanded.

With the screaming of the kids and the cawing of the birds, April couldn't hear Eve. "Huh?"

"Come on! You're slower than a Sunday afternoon." Eve grabbed April's arm and yanked her to her feet.

"A what?" Grace asked as she reached for April's other arm.

"It means get moving! Get in the classroom. Go! GO!" Eve sounded like a drill sergeant.

The girls bolted through the doorway, and slammed the door behind them. Looking around, they saw a few other kids who had also made it to safety.

Outside the door, kids ran by, tripping and screaming in the hallway. As knocks sounded on the door, Grace and another boy were careful to let in kids without letting in any birds. One girl limped into the classroom with her hand on her knee. Another shuffled in, holding her head. April thought, *Oh no! Everyone is getting hurt.*

In the classroom, kids chattered about the chaos, the mess and the bird poop everywhere. April sat, holding her head in her hands. Then a chill went up her back again and a strange feeling came over her. *Something else is wrong.* She stood up. Her eyes searched the classroom. *What is this feeling? Why does it feel like someone is watching me?*

She crept toward the classroom door and peered out the window. Mr. Malus was there, staring back at her with his cold, dark eyes. He just stood there as kids ran by him, birds flew over his head, and teachers yelled. His eyes stayed fixed on April. His gaze made April's face feel hotter. *Why is he staring at me like that? Something isn't right. I've got to find out what's happening.*

April's heart beat so fast and hard that she could feel it in her throat. She went to open the door. But he quickly turned around and walked to the side door that led out to some stairs.

At that moment, David called out to her. "April!"

She turned to look at him. He laughed. His cackle reminded her of those spooky mechanical witches in store displays.

The beads of sweat on April's nose caused her glasses to slide down again. She pushed them back up with shaking hands. *What is going on? His voice sounds so weird. What should I do? Think. Think!*

CHAPTER 8

DAVID stopped laughing. The smile on his face disappeared. He threw up his arms again and said, “Freeze!”

Everything and everyone stopped. April’s eyes scanned the room of frozen fifth graders. It was like a game of freeze-tag, everyone was as still as a statue. “It’s just you and me now,” he said in that same creepy voice.

As noisy as everything had been a few moments ago, it was quiet now. The only thing she heard was the whistling heaters and the caws of the crows. The screams of the kids were silenced. David took a step toward her. April looked over her shoulder at Grace and Eve. "Help!" she cried out to them. But they weren't moving. Grace was frozen, drinking the water bottle she had pulled out of her book bag earlier. Eve was perfectly still, glaring suspiciously at David.

"The Jokester and the Southern Belle aren't witches. They can't save you. I can freeze time on them." He took another step closer to April and laughed again.

OMG...what has he done to my friends—to everyone? A lump grew in her throat. Her hands shook. *I don't want anyone else to get hurt. I don't want anyone else to be scared. What do I do? What do I do?*

April dropped her book bag and ran out of the classroom. She ran around kids frozen in place. Next door to her classroom was the girls' bathroom. She pushed open the door, went in and leaned her back against it. She put her head back onto the door and closed her eyes as tears streamed down her face.

She brushed the tears away angrily. *I can't cry now. I have to figure out how to fix this. Mom says there is no space in your heart for fear. But, WHAT AM I SUPPOSED TO DO?*

April slid down the door in despair, staring at the floor. The stress of last night and this morning had finally gotten to her.

"Help me, someone. Help me," she whispered.

"April, you have to listen up now."

The voice was from a woman with a Southern accent. It came from somewhere in front of her. April jumped to her feet. A blurry shadow appeared. Her glasses had smudges and tears covering them. She wiped the lenses with a dry corner of her shirt.

When she put them back on, she saw an older woman standing there. She was wearing a beautiful, light blue dress with a white lace shawl draped over her shoulders. Her long, dark, curly hair was streaked with gray and hung down her back. Her smooth, caramel skin glowed.

April blinked her eyes hard. *OMG...who is she? Am I imagining this?* She pinched herself. "Ouch!"

"*Pauve ti bête*, bless your heart. You pinched yourself to see if this was real or a dream."

April nodded her head. The woman's sweet, grandmotherly voice made April feel calmer.

"Oh, honey pie. I'm Eve's *grand-mère.* Call me Josephine." Her Cajun accent was the same as Eve's and it made April smile. *That's right! Eve's grandmother had given Eve the* Book of Magie *before she passed away. Boy, if my friends thought I had seen a ghost before, wait till they hear about this!*

"Listen up now, we don't have much time. I've got a lot to tell ya but we don't have all day now." She spoke quickly. "For hundreds of years, good witches passed their spell books to other good witches. I made sure that the *Book of Magie* made its way to you. Since you have my spell book you also have me."

April tilted her head and raised an eyebrow.

"Any time ya ask for help I'll be there. Think of me as your Fairy Godmother, like Cinderella." Josephine flashed her a sweet smile.

"Good witches help other good witches. If you are really distressed and need help, jus' call me. But, I am not your genie in a bottle. You don't call me unless you really need me." Josephine put her hands on her hips.

"I—I think David's a bad witch. He ruined my dad's car, called those birds and froze time. Plus, he has this evil laugh that gives me chills," April said.

Josephine's eyebrows furrowed and her eyes narrowed. "Honey child, think back to what happened. Was David evil all the time? Or, was there something or someone that might have triggered this behavior in David. Like a word or sound?" Josephine inquired.

April thought about that for a moment. "When Grace slipped, David helped her up; he was so sweet and charming. Then when Mr. Malus clapped his hands, everything about David changed: his voice, his laugh, even the way his face looks." April tapped her finger on her cheek and paced in the bathroom. "So, is Mr. Malus controlling David?"

CHAPTER 9

"SLOW down now, we'll get to that," Josephine looked at the heater in the bathroom. "Now, let's start from where the evil spells began. First was the heat, then these birds, right?" Josephine gestured at the bathroom door, as the caws from the crows continued.

"Yes," said April. "And the freezing time thing. This is really freaking me out."

"Oh, I remember the first time a *Logisilld* tried to scare me." Josephine looked off into the distance. "Those can be tense moments but nothing ya can't handle."

"A *Logisilld*? What's that?"

Josephine looked up and to the right. "Oh, that's an evil witch that can make other people do things that they may not have the powers to do themselves. Maybe Monsieur Malus can't freeze time on his own, or maybe he can. But, he found David and for some reason is using him to do it."

"What?" April's hands shook.

"Oh, honey, calm yourself. Just keep reading the *Book of Magie*. You'll learn more about this as time goes on. We don't have time for a full lesson right now. Just you focus on getting rid of this heat and sending the birds back to their nests. April, dear, it will all be okay. There is no space in your heart for fear." Josephine beamed.

"My mom says that same exact thing."

"She is a wise woman." Josephine winked. "Now, to the heat. I want you to place the palms of your hands over the radiator—but don't touch it, it's hot—and say,

Heat go back to normal,
Take this request as formal.
Turn down, turn down to cool.
And, circulate the air around the school.

"Okay," April placed both palms a few inches over the radiator and repeated the spell.

Heat go back to normal,
Take this request as formal.
Turn down, turn down to cool.
And, circulate the air around the school.

The heater stopped hissing. April walked over to the door and pressed her ear against it.

The hissing also stopped in the hallway.

April heard footsteps coming down the hall.

Stomp, stomp, stomp. Boots approached the door. "That little goody-two-shoes witch is undoing my spell."

That's not David. April swallowed the lump in her throat.

Josephine said, "That's not David, my dear. David is not evil. He's being controlled."

April's face grew hot and her heart pounded. "That is Mr. Malus. Mr. Malus is an evil witch that is controlling David!"

CHAPTER 10

APRIL'S heart pounded so hard her body shook. *Mr. Malus is controlling David!* Her head swirled and the room spun. *Could he control me too?* She took a deep breath and steadied herself.

The footsteps approached the bathroom door. "April, dear, we have to work quickly. It is you who must say the spell. Repeat after me to get the crows out of the building."

Fly home ye crows,
For you are not my foes.
In the sky, ye shall roam,
Swoop around and fly home.

April pressed her back against the door and closed her eyes as she repeated again:

Fly home ye crows,
For you are not my foes.
In the sky, ye shall roam,
Swoop around and fly home.

She pressed her ear to the door. *Are the crows gone*?

"Noooo! David, come!" Mr. Malus called. "They are flying away!"

April cracked open the bathroom door to peek into the hallway. Mr. Malus was running down the hall when *SWOOSH!* a crow swooped down. Mr. Malus ducked but tripped over someone's textbook. *BAM!* He fell on his bottom. "Ouch!" he yelled.

David helped him up while crows flew over their heads and out the front doors of the school. Then another one swooped down toward his head and *PLOP!* White bird poop dripped from Mr. Malus's head. April tried to hold in a giggle but she didn't catch it in time. A small guffaw came out.

David and Mr. Malus's eyes met April's as she looked out the door. April slammed the door closed. Leaning against it, she said, "They know I'm here and they're coming. What should I do?"

She turned her head to the left and to the right. There was no one. "Josephine, where did you go?"

A sweet, faint, Cajun-accented voice said, "You can handle this now. Remember, there is no space in your heart for fear."

April squeezed her eyes closed. *I can do this. I WILL do this!* She took a deep breath and opened her eyes. There it was. Her escape.

The bathroom window.

CHAPTER 11

EXCITEMENT bubbled up inside her.

The sink was bolted to the wall under the window. April put one foot on the sink and pushed herself up. Balancing carefully, she pressed up on the window and it opened.

She could only get half of her body through the window while standing on the sink, so she used her arms to push herself through. *Oomph!* She fell a few feet and landed on the grass, knocking the wind out of herself.

She lay on the ground under the window trying to catch her breath. *BOOM!* The bathroom door flew open and hit the wall.

"Where did that little twerp go?" Mr. Malus asked.

Creak. Bang. Creak. Bang. The bathroom stall doors were pushed open and slammed against the walls. *They are looking for me. I have to get out of here.*

David's voice sounded like it did when he helped Grace. "She really isn't that bad. She was so concerned about her friend when she fell and about the heat being messed up and—"

CLAP-CLAP. The thunderous clap of Mr. Malus's hands echoed in the bathroom.

"WE must get April Appleton. Do you hear me? Now repeat it," Mr. Malus commanded.

"We must get April Appleton," David said. His voice changed. He sounded like a robot again. Josephine was right. Mr. Malus was certainly controlling David.

Mr. Malus continued in a low voice, "You must get her so I can take her back with me where we will take her powers." He let out an evil chuckle.

April's heart thumped. *Back? To where? We? Who is we?*

At the end of the school yard, before the sidewalk, stood the bike racks. *Bingo, Austin's bike! Yes!*

She jumped to her feet. Her heart pounded so hard it felt like it would pop out of her chest. She ran toward the bike.

"There she is!" David yelled.

She whipped her head around and saw David's head sticking out of the bathroom window.

OMG…I have to get out of here. Run, run!

CHAPTER 12

APRIL reached the bike rack. She grabbed Austin's lock. *Please, please, please, Austin, I hope you didn't change your password.* Using her thumb, she clicked the numbers until they got to his password 0-4-0-9, his birthday. She yanked the lock and it popped off.

Meanwhile, David shimmied out of the window. He fell onto the grass, landing on his head.

Mr. Malus screamed, "Go get her! I can't fit through this window. Hold her. I will find you!"

OMG...I have to get out of here! She swung her leg over the top of the bike but her foot couldn't reach the ground. Austin was at least five inches taller than her. She fumbled until her foot found the pedal.

She gave a big jump and a push to start it rolling and hopped onto the bike. David stood only a few feet away. April pumped the pedals as hard as she could, going faster and faster down the sidewalk.

She turned her head. David searched for an unlocked bike. Her bike wobbled and she whipped her head around to face forward. Righting herself, April dared to take one more look. David managed to find a bike and was pedaling like mad to catch up to her.

Every muscle in her legs squeezed and pressed to make the bike go as fast as it could. *He's gaining on me. Pedal harder. Pedal faster!*

April's heart thumped. Her palms were wet

with sweat. Then, Josephine's words came back to her: '*You can handle this now. Remember there is no space in your heart for fear.*' *I can't be afraid. I can handle this. What spells do I remember from the* Book of Magie?

She arrived at her house. Her father's crushed car was gone. She flew up the driveway and stopped at the side door to the kitchen. The bike fell as her feet hit the ground. April dug in her pocket and pulled out the house key. David rode up the driveway on the stolen bicycle.

April stepped through the door into the kitchen and tried to close it behind her. But David wedged his body in between the door and the frame and she couldn't shut it.

He laughed a creepy, evil laugh. "I'm bringing you to Mr. Malus," he said.

April knew she couldn't match his strength and backed away into the kitchen.

He opened the door fully and entered the

house. "He's going to take you back with him."

David walked closer to April. "Oh, you think Mr. Malus didn't know you undid the spell of the branch that fell on your father's car? I came back last night and made sure the branch fell again. And that it stayed there. Now, come here so I can bring you to him." He reached out and grabbed April's arm.

She held her breath. Her heart raced. April had never been so scared. *Do something. What's in the* Book of Magie? *Remember something. Remember anything!*

I've got it! I know a spell that turns someone back to normal. I know I've seen it in the Book of Magie!

CHAPTER 13

THE spell in the *Book of Magie* flashed before her eyes. *That's right. I need two things: an article of clothing, and a strand of hair.*

She tore at the front of David's shirt with her free hand and pulled as hard as she could, ripping a few buttons off. An article of clothing. *Check.*

David tried to grab her other hand. April reached for his ponytail. YANK! A few strands of hair came loose. *Check.*

"Ouch!" David yelled and felt his head.

She stepped back. *I just need a second to be able to say it without him getting me.* "Josephine, please help."

David tried to grab her arm but somehow tripped, falling onto the kitchen floor. April thanked Josephine silently and stepped further back. Squeezing her eyes shut, she said:

"Heaven please help with the recent past,
To un-do the spell that was just cast.
Please take this request as formal,
And, turn David back to normal."

She squeezed her eyes tighter and raised her shoulders up toward her ears. She cracked one eye open. *Please let it work.*

"Why am I here?" David asked. "April, is that you? Am I in your house?" His eyes scanned her kitchen.

The tone of his voice was different. It was his normal voice. He looked down and noticed his ripped shirt with the missing buttons. His eyes moved to what April was holding. "Why—what—? You are as red as a cardinal. What's going on?"

"David, do you know Mr. Malus?"

"Yeah. He's our math teacher. Yesterday afternoon, I went to him after school to ask if I could do extra credit to raise my grade. He's super mean," David recalled.

April exhaled. "I've heard that before."

"Funny, I don't remember much after that." David sat down on one of the stools on the other side of the kitchen counter. He blinked as he looked at the ground, obviously trying to piece things together.

April walked toward the kitchen island and rested her elbows on it with her chin in her hands. "Think hard. What do you remember?"

"Oh, I remember helping Grace up when she slipped and fell on the hallway floor. I told her to be careful." He cleared his throat and looked down at the ground again.

"David, do you remember anything else?"

"No." David's eyes met April's.

"Do you remember coming to my house and breaking a big branch off our tree out there?" April pointed out the door.

"What? I'd never ever do that! I'm learning how to help plants, animals, and people, not harm them!" David's jaw tightened.

"Really? What are you learning? Are you also a witch?"

CHAPTER 14

DAVID cleared his throat then dropped his head. "No, not really. I'm a medicine man in training. Like a healer."

He put his hand in his jeans pocket and pulled out a small, beaded leather pouch. "Here are some of the herbs my grandfather is teaching me about right now. My family has many medicine people and—wait, you asked if I am 'also' a witch. April, are you a witch?"

"Well, it's kind of a long story but I, um, I

have these powers. And, I have this book—"

"Sorry to interrupt—but what's up with the mailman?" David pointed out the kitchen window and jumped to his feet. The mailman stood frozen on the sidewalk across the street. His large mail bag hung limply.

"Oh," April gave a nervous chuckle. "I didn't get to that part yet. So…you froze time." April looked at David carefully.

His eyes widened. "I did WHAT?"

"I know. It's really freaky and I'm trying to be calm. Maybe Mr. Malus does not have his own power to freeze time but he found you and, uh, I guess you do."

"I can what?" David asked again as he squeezed his eyes shut.

Poor David, he has no clue of all the trouble he caused. "We can figure out more later. Right now, like I was saying, I have this spell book upstairs."

David slowly backed away from April. "Uh, I don't mess around with that stuff." He took another step backward. "From the stories my grandfather and father tell me, witches are people that have been cursed."

April stopped in surprise and she focused on David. "Actually, I think my powers have been a blessing. A gift. Yeah, sometimes they can cause some problems but they can also help me fix things. You know?"

David raised an eyebrow and tilted his head. Suspicion covered his face.

April continued, "Maybe Mr. Malus made you do all those bad things."

"What do you mean, *all* those bad things?' "

"You, or him, or both of you, jacked up the heat at school and made a flock of crows fly through it, pooping everywhere, then you froze time. And, I'm pretty sure that you are the one that caused the tree branch to crush my father's car." April bit her lower lip.

David narrowed his eyes as he looked out the window. "You know what? The last thing I remember was being in Mr. Malus's classroom. I wonder if he cursed me?"

"I noticed when he clapped his hands and rubbed the charm on his necklace, you'd change," April added.

"Change how?"

"Well, you just seemed different. Earlier, when you helped Grace up, you were so nice. After he clapped his hands, your face was just blank and you had this horrible robotic laugh."

David's eyes bulged and his nostrils flared.

"But, I was able to do a spell to lift the curse Mr. Malus put on you," April said.

David exhaled. "Wow, my sister calls me evil sometimes but that's for scaring her with fake spiders and, this one time—I set a bunch of alarm clocks for different times in the middle of the night and hid them around her room so she couldn't find them when they went off!"

David let out a big belly laugh. His normal laugh made April smile. "She was mad at me for days." He continued to chuckle.

"You would get along really well with my brother, Austin," she rolled her eyes. "But, like I was saying, I have a book that helps me do *good* spells. And, we could look at it to see what we can do about Mr. Malus."

"We? No, no." David shook his head. "*You* are the witch. I'm just learning how to heal and help people, like my father, grandfather, and great-grandfather."

"Uh-huh, just come on. I'm sure Mr. Malus is wondering where you are." April grabbed David's hand and pulled him through the dining room and up the stairs.

CHAPTER 15

APRIL walked into her bedroom. David stood in the doorway, like he was paralyzed. She knelt on the carpet next to her bed. She pulled the heavy book out, sliding it across her pink carpet. "This is the *Book of Magie*," April said as she turned toward David.

He did not move. After a deep breath, he slowly walked into her room. Sitting on the carpet behind her, he peered over her shoulder as if the book was going to attack him.

"It's so old." He pointed at the title. "What is *Magie*?"

"It means magic in French. I had to learn French to be able to do the spells. Good spells, you know, to help with different things, like... lifting your curse." She smiled at him.

"I'm not touching it." David pointed at the book again and jerked his head back, making a face like he had smelled poop. "I can't believe I'm in the same room as it," he murmured.

"Oh, calm down, you have powers too; after all, you're the one who made the branch fall and the birds attack! But you can figure all that out later, I have to find the spell. You just sit there." April told him.

"Yeah, well, I don't speak French, either." David said. He still looked nervous.

April felt a bit sorry for him; after all, being a witch is difficult. She opened the front cover and turned the thin pages. "This is the first spell I did." She pointed at the picture of a woman standing with an animal.

"What's that?"

"It's a spell to turn someone into an animal. I turned my pestering older brother into a cute, white, fluffy dog." She shrugged her shoulders.

"Not something gross like a centipede or a spider?"

April wrinkled her nose. "Ew! No."

David chuckled, his worry disappearing.

She hunched back over the book scanning the pages in search of the right spell.

"By the way, thank you, Good Witch, for removing the curse." David smiled at April.

"No problem. Any time. 'Good Witch?'" April asked and raised an eyebrow.

"I give all of my friends nicknames. Hm, maybe not Good Witch because I don't want to give away our secrets in school." He winked. "Maybe Glenda, from *The Wizard of Oz*? Or,

Hermione. From *Harry Potter*."

He's really nice. I knew it. April looked up and smiled at him.

Creeeaaaakkk. BANG! The kitchen screen door slammed shut.

They both looked toward April's bedroom door. The tremble in April's hands came back. "Oh no, we left the door open and the bikes in front of the house, didn't we?" April asked in a quiet voice.

"Who's here?" David whispered.

April looked at him. "It can only be one person because everyone else is frozen..."

"Mr. Malus," they said at the same time.

The hardwood floors downstairs creaked as Mr. Malus took a step toward the stairs. A bead of sweat formed on her forehead. *Creak*. The creaks got louder as he climbed each step. She swallowed hard.

"I have a plan," David said with a smile. "Follow my lead."

CHAPTER 16

WHAT'S *he going to do? I hope he's got a good plan.*

David took a deep breath, lifted and raised his shoulders, then erased the smile from his face. His frown reminded her of the look he had back at school. April gasped. *Is he pretending to be under Mr. Malus's spell?*

"Don't worry. Play along," David whispered out of the corner of his mouth. He pointed under the bed, directing her to hide. He walked out of the bedroom toward the stairs. April pushed the book under her bed and crawled under with it. She laid on the book, holding it tightly. She could hear them talking.

"Where is the little goody-two-shoes witch?" Mr. Malus asked. His gruff voice reminded her of pirates from movies. She saw David and Mr. Malus's skinny legs as they stood in the hall.

"I can't find her," David responded, sounding like a robot. *He's playing along so well.*

Mr. Malus walked past him and looked into her parents' bedroom. Then he walked to the next door to Austin's room. He opened the door. "Ugh, what a smell!" He closed the door then took another step. "Her room has to be up here somewhere. The other *Logisilld* said she and that book would be there."

April's hands shook as she held the book. *OMG! That's the word Josephine used.* April squeezed the book tighter. His worn, dark brown boots stomped back down the hall toward her room. Her heart raced.

"She has to be here. Her bike is out front. I didn't come three hundred years into the future to go back empty-handed. Come out, come out, wherever you are," he sing-songed as he walked past the bathroom and into April's room.

"A Logi-what?" David asked.

"Simple boy, I am a *Logisilld*, an ancient wizard from centuries ago. I came here to this time to get that *Book of Magie* and to use the girl's powers, just as I've used yours. But, maybe I'll take her back with me, too. Josephine—that old witch—kept that book hidden from us. When we would finally find it, she'd somehow sneak it away and hide it again!" Mr. Malus opened April's closet door. He pushed some clothes around.

"You see, we had an idea that the book was here. I tricked everyone into thinking I was a math teacher so I could study April and find out where that book was. But by a stroke of luck, I discovered you and your great powers! Now I didn't have to do this all on my own and risk getting caught. So, I had you break the branch to fall on her father's car so he couldn't give her a ride to school. But then she fixed it! I had you come back, freeze time so she wouldn't hear anything and make it fall again!"

Mr. Malus laughed an evil laugh. "I needed her to get to school a little later so I could keep you under my curse to set up the distractions of the heat and birds. I thought she would bring the book with her to keep it safe, given all the troubles at home. However, she keeps surprising me. I'm sure that ghost-witch, Josephine, has tipped her off," he grumbled.

He knows Josephine? How? Why?

Mr. Malus looked under her desk.

April stopped breathing. *He's going to find*

me! He stood back up. She exhaled but could not stop her lips from quivering. So many thoughts rushed through her mind. *Was it the spell I did that broke David's curse or some power Josephine gave me? What else can I do? How can I get us out of this?*

"She's here. I can tell." He paced back and forth in her room. Then he stopped. His dirty boots stood two feet in front of her. Her glasses slid down to the tip of her nose. The bottom rim rested on the book.

April swallowed hard, squeezed her eyes shut and tightened her whole body. *He wants to take my powers. How is he going to do that? I thought they were a gift. Maybe they are a curse. What can I do?*

She took a deep breath. The lump in her throat grew as she opened her eyes to find Mr. Malus's thin face not twelve inches from hers.

CHAPTER 17

"FOUND you! Time to come out now," Mr. Malus sneered. His yellow, crooked teeth looked like they hadn't been brushed in months, or ever. "And bring the book with you."

April crawled out from under the bed, clutching the large book close to her chest. She sat on the rug with her back against the bed. Mr. Malus rubbed the quarter-sized charm on his necklace between his fingers.

He's going to do another spell!

“First, I must un-freeze time so that I may bring you back with me.” His high-pitched, evil cackle made April’s ears burn. She covered them with both hands, letting the book fall to her lap. *No, I don’t want to leave! I will miss my mom and dad. I will even miss Austin. My powers aren’t a gift, they’re a curse. Josephine, where are you? Help me!* April closed her eyes as tears fell down her cheeks.

Mr. Malus closed his eyes.

“Tick-tock,
Forward the clock.
Time shall move and go,
Forward on, forever so.”

April looked at the clock on her wall. The second hand was moving again. She looked at David, who stood behind Mr. Malus. The whole time he just stared at his feet. Then, he quickly looked up at April. His face brightened and the corners of his mouth rose. He slid his hand into his pocket as he winked at April. Flicking his eyes toward the open closet door, he raised his eyebrows.

What is he doing? Is he trying to tell me something?

A wicked smile appeared on Mr. Malus's face. His eyes opened. "Now, time for us to go. The others will be so pleased." He couldn't take his eyes off the spell book. He stared at it like April's dad stared at a grilled steak. He rubbed his charm between his fingers and took a deep breath.

"Back in time we go..."

Just then, David pulled a handful of his herbs out of his pocket and threw them at the teacher's face. Mr. Malus squeezed his eyes shut and swung his arm. "No! Where are you? Ouch! This stings!" He tried to wipe the herbs out of his eyes with one hand and reached out to grab David with the other.

David ducked. "April! Help me get him into the closet!"

April jumped to her feet and shoved Mr. Malus backward into the closet as he reached out blindly. Together they gave one last push and Mr. Malus fell on the floor of the closet.

David slammed the door and sat in front of the closet. He put his feet on the ground, pressing his back against the door.

David asked, "So, from one witch to another, is there anything you can find in that book to send him back to where he came from?"

CHAPTER 18

APRIL grabbed the book and sat with her back against the door helping David hold it shut.

Mr. Malus yelled and banged on the door. "My eyes! I will get you. You will pay for this!"

"Um, can you find something? He might be skinny, but I don't think we can hold him much longer." David said, digging his heels into April's rug.

April flipped one page after another. "It is a three-hundred-year-old book. It doesn't have a table of contents," April quipped.

Mr. Malus continued pounding on the door, making it difficult for April to keep the book steady on her lap.

"Found it!" April yelled. Mr. Malus stopped banging. There was only silence as she read:

"Tick-tock, Backward the clock.
Three hundred years, goeth back
Land in the bygone days,
Land there where he stays."

David looked at April. April looked at David. "Did it work?" David asked.

They inched away from the door and slowly got to their feet.

BAM! Mr. Malus kicked the door open. "You stupid, young witch, you're not capable of doing magic on me."

April stopped breathing. The blood rushed out of her face. *What do I do?*

"Josephine, help!"

"That ghost-witch can't help you! I'm taking you back." He lunged at April. She ducked and ran to the other side of the room. "You're a quick little thing; you will be helpful to us in many ways." His roaring laugh filled the room.

The faint, accented voice of Josephine whispered in April's ear, "The book is your key. Hold it, point it at him and say it again. That's why they want you, they need the book. It gives the owner power over other witches."

Mr. Malus turned around to face April. He charged forward. April darted to the side and slid onto the floor, grabbing the book. She wrapped her arm around it, laying on the ground. Rising to her knees and pointing the book at him, she said:

"Tick-tock, Backward the clock.
Three hundred years, goeth back
Land in the bygone days,
Land there where he stays."

Poof! April watched as a puff of smoke appeared and Mr. Malus vanished.

She exhaled. The book thumped to the floor as she let go of it. "Thank you, Josephine."

"You're welcome, my dear," Josephine whispered.

"Who are you talking to? Who's Josephine?" David asked. He turned to the right then turned to the left. "Do you see someone I don't?"

"Never mind." April flopped onto the rug, putting her head down on the book like it was a pillow.

Tick-tock. Tick-tock. Her clock quietly ticked. April jolted up. "Oh, wow! Time is moving forward again, we have to get back to school."

April pushed the *Book of Magie* safely back under her bed.

CHAPTER 19

THEY ran down the stairs, through the dining room and out of the kitchen door, locking it behind them.

"We have to get back to school now!" David said as he jumped onto the bike.

They pedaled hard and fast. By the time they got to school, April was gasping for air. They glided up to the bike rack. April nearly fell off Austin's large bike. She then re-chained it to the rack.

"Where was this bike from?" David asked.

April shrugged her shoulders.

David looked puzzled. "I don't remember." He stared at the bikes in the rack. "I'll just leave it on the side." He leaned it against the bike rack.

April walked down the side of the school to the bathroom window. She motioned for David to follow her. She stopped in front of it and pointed. "We have to go in that way."

David opened his eyes wide. "Why?"

April pointed. "Because they're going in the front door."

A group of men were approaching the school's front door. Their voices grew louder. One said, "We better get in there fast. The principal called and said it was urgent."

"Go, go, go," April said in a hushed whisper.

"Okay. I'll go feet first." David sat on the windowsill with his legs dangling inside. He slid into the bathroom and landed on his bottom in the sink. "Oomph!"

"You all right?" April asked.

"I've been better but I'll live." He looked around. "So, this is what the girls' bathroom looks like!"

April said, "Come on, David, stop fooling around, those men are coming!"

David reached out to help April climb in. "Come on."

She quickly hopped down to the floor and walked to the door, reaching for the handle.

"Wait!" David stopped her from opening the door. "We can't come out together. I mean, I shouldn't even be in here at all!"

April heard the click-tap of a woman's high-heeled shoes echo from the hall. The click-tap went back and forth in front of the bathroom door. "You're right. I'll go out first and wait until it is all clear, then let you out. Okay?"

She stepped out of the bathroom and into

the hall. It was still hot and there was bird poop, feathers, backpacks, and papers all over the floor.

"April! What are you doing out of your classroom?" April's heart raced. She swallowed hard. *OMG! OMG! I know that voice. It's Principal Ramirez!*

CHAPTER 20

APRIL bit her lower lip. *Think fast. You can do this.*

Mrs. Ramirez focused on April. "I told everyone to wait in their classrooms until either their parent or their bus arrives."

"Huh, you did?" April asked.

"Yes, I made the announcement over the loud speaker that we are dismissing school early because of the heat issue and that weird bird invasion. Even though things seem to be fine now, we have to make sure that the pipes are working properly and that there are no more birds in the building. You have to get back to your classroom right now so—"

"Mrs. Ramirez! Mrs. Ramirez!" A voice called from close to the front door. It was Mrs. Chen, the school secretary. She waved her thin arms up and down. "The repair people are here to look at the heat pipes!" She yelled down the hall.

"Oh, thank goodness! April, go back to your classroom now. I don't want anyone else getting hurt." Mrs. Ramirez turned around abruptly and walked toward Mrs. Chen.

Mrs. Ramirez walked the plumbers to the front staircase. Mrs. Chen took quick little steps back into the main office. April looked up and down the hall. *No one.* She exhaled. "Come on out." She pushed the door open.

David rushed out of the bathroom. "Ew. I

think the girls' bathroom smells worse than the boys'!" He pinched his nose. April grabbed his arm and pulled him down the hall to their classroom.

Over the loud speaker, Mrs. Chen said, "Children on buses one, five and six, please walk slowly down the hall. Your buses are here."

Their teacher was busy attending to kids who looked like they were hurt. She didn't even notice that April and David were back in the classroom, or that they were missing at all. April picked up her book bag which was in the same place she dropped it. "I better go. They called my bus."

April leaned in close to David's ear and said, "Great job today, Medicine Man."

David smiled. "Thanks, Glenda."

April walked out of the classroom right into Grace and Eve. Eve gasped, "Where have you been? And, where did David disappear to? I'm *sure* you know."

Grace narrowed her eyes. April smiled and laughed nervously as they walked down the hall toward the doors. "Well, it's a long story."

"I'm sure it is." Grace's voice had a suspicious tone.

April leaned closer to the girls. "I have so much to tell you." They walked to their bus. "But, I don't want to say anything now." April looked sideways at the other kids.

"Oh, right." Eve nodded. "I called my mom and she said I can go to Grace's house."

As they reached the bus, April heard someone calling her name. She looked across the street and saw a shiny black SUV with big, sparkly wheels. Her dad sat in the front seat, waving at her out of the window. "I came to pick you up," he called.

April turned to her friends who were boarding the bus. "Hey, come to my house when you get off of the bus. I'll get home before you and

I'll make us a snack."

"Okay," Grace and Eve said at the same time.

"You *have* to tell us everything," Eve said.

"For sure." April smiled and nodded. She walked to the crosswalk where the crossing guard stopped traffic for the students.

April walked up to the big car, opened the back door and hopped in. "Wow, Dad, what is this?"

"It's the loaner car that the insurance company gave me." Her dad grinned.

April ran her hand down the soft leather seat and door panel. "How do you like it?"

"I love it! I think I found my *new* dream car." Her dad looked in the rearview mirror and gave her a wink.

She looked out the window and took a deep breath. Thinking about everything that happened, she pondered how David had discovered that he was also a witch. It made her think about how far she had come since the day she discovered her own powers.

Josephine, thanks for everything today. I couldn't have done it without you.

A faint whisper in her ear said, "Oh, honey pie, you were the one who remembered that there is no space in your heart for fear. You found the strength and you did it all yourself."

April sat back in the seat and watched the neighborhood roll by, smiling to herself and wondering what her next magical adventure might be.

ABOUT THE AUTHOR

Talia Aikens-Nuñez dreamed of being a meteorologist as a child because her head was always in the clouds. It was her imagination and her fun-loving, second-grade daughter that inspired her to write her OMG books about an accidental little witch. She and her husband live on a river in Connecticut with their daughter and son.

Talia's other books include:

OMG... Am I a Witch?!

OMG... I Did It Again?!

Escucha Means Listen